Bebop Express

Special Thanks to
Twin City Model Railroad Museum, Minnesota Transportation Museum,
Via's Vintage Wear, and Joe, Ron, Ethel, Michael, Vincent, and Josie.

Library of Congress Cataloging-in-Publication Data
Panahi, H. L. (Heather L.)
Bebop Express / by H. L. Panahi ; illustrated by Steve Johnson and Lou Fancher. —
1st ed.
   p.   cm.
   Summary: A rollicking rhythmic express train takes passengers on a jazzy
journey that celebrates the United States and its unique musical culture.
   ISBN 0-06-057190-X — ISBN 0-06-057191-8 (lib. bdg.)
   [1. Railroads—Trains—Fiction.   2. Jazz—Fiction.   3. Stories in rhyme.]
I. Johnson, Steve, date, ill.   II. Fancher, Lou, ill.   III. Title.
PZ8.3.P1573Be 2005
[E]—dc22
                                                        2003024244
                                                             CIP
                                                             AC

Book Design by Lou Fancher
1 2 3 4 5 6 7 8 9 10
❖
First Edition

To Shahriar, Nora, and Maya—
You make my life a groovin' and movin',
nonstoppin' boppin' adventure.
—H.L.P.

To our family and friends,
who bebop on these pages.
—S.J. & L.F.

BebOP ExpReSS

by H. L. Panahi

illustrated by **Steve Johnson** and **Lou Fancher**

LAURA GERINGER BOOKS
An Imprint of HarperCollins Publishers

Amistad

The whistle's a-blowin', the engine's a-pumpin'—
conductors are dancin' and passengers jumpin'!
Quick! Climb aboard the Bebop Express.
It's the jazziest train from the east to the west.
Chug-a chug-a chug-a chug-a Choo! Choo!
Chug-a chug-a chug-a chug-a Choo! Choo!

From New York's train station the trip will begin.

Can you hear that cool sound risin' up from the din?

Sax Man is here with his shiny brass horn,

where magical, jazzical music is born.

His horn says blee blee, doot doot wah!
Blee blah, blee blah, doot doot bah!
He blows it, blasts it, swings it, sways it;
everybody grooves when Sax Man plays it.

Chug-a chug-a chug-a chug-a
Choo! Choo!
Chug-a chug-a chug-a chug-a
Choo! Choo!

Next stop is Philly, at Thirtieth Street, where
DRUM MAN is keepin' a slam-jammin' beat.
With sticks in his hands he flails and he wails,
he drums on the walls and the big garbage pails.

Rat-a-tat, rat-a-tat. **BLAM! BOP! BLAM!**

Boom chicka, boom chicka. **WHAM! KER-SLAM!**

He hits it, dips it, rolls it, flips it. No one can touch him when he rips it.

Chug-a chug-a chug-a chug-a Choo! Choo!

Chug-a chug-a chug-a chug-a Choo! Choo!

On to Chicago, the great Windy City.
The jazz here is spunky and funky and gritty.
In a long black coat, with shades on his face,
one Happenin' Cat plays the BEBOPPIN' BASS.

Ba doom, ba doom, ba doom. Dow! Dow!

Plink, plink, doom ba doom. Pow! Pow!

He plinks it, plucks it, spins it, drums it,

snaps and pops it while he strums it.

Chug-a chug-a chug-a chug-a
Choo! Choo!
Chug-a chug-a chug-a chug-a
Choo! Choo!

Right in St. Louis, around Forest Park,

we'll pick up a lady who sings like a lark.

Song Lady's voice is as smooth as fine silk—

riffs glide from her lips just like rich buttermilk.

Oooh wee ooh. Bop! She-bop!
La tee dah. Doo-wop! Doo-wop!
She hums it, speaks it, sings it, swoons it,
scats and bebops while she croons it.
Chug-a chug-a chug-a chug-a
Choo! Choo!
Chug-a chug-a chug-a chug-a
Choo! Choo!

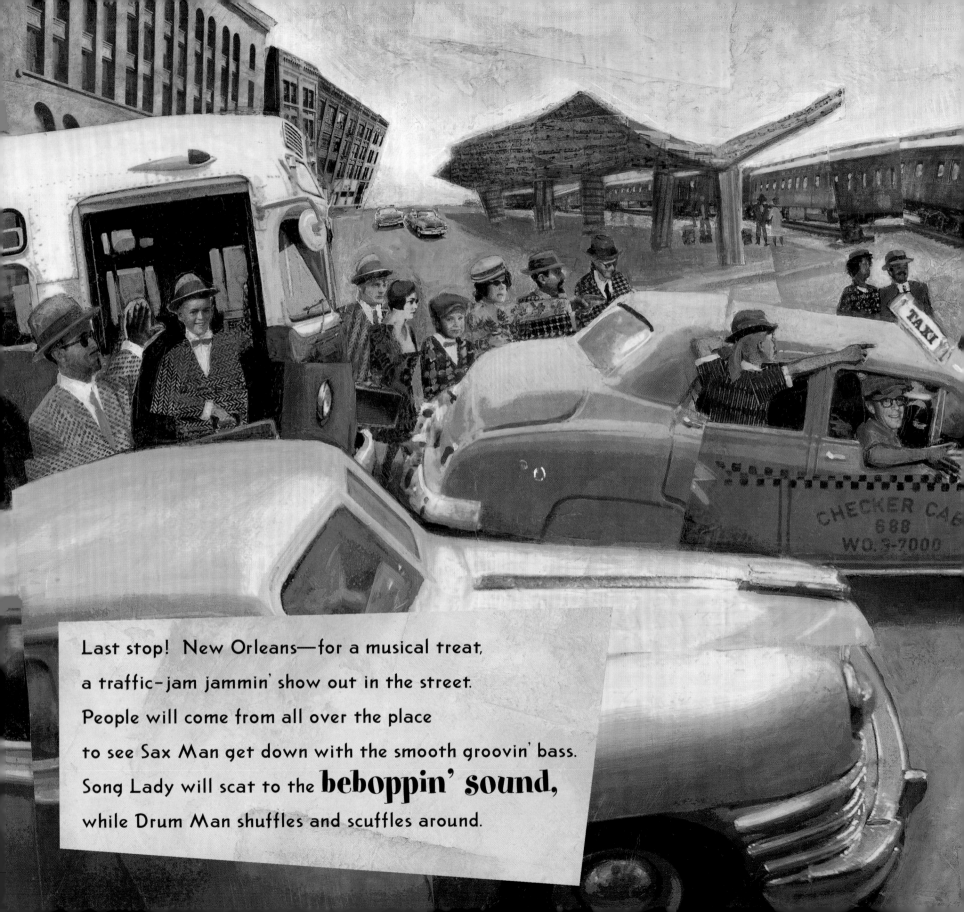

Last stop! New Orleans—for a musical treat,
a traffic-jam jammin' show out in the street.
People will come from all over the place
to see Sax Man get down with the smooth groovin' bass.
Song Lady will scat to the **beboppin' sound,**
while Drum Man shuffles and scuffles around.

They'll be skippin' it, rippin' it,
hummin' and drummin' it,
slappin' it, tappin' it,
finger-and-**thumbin'** it,
flailin' and wailin' it,
swingin' and swayin' it.
People will clap along
while they are **playin'** it.

Blee bah, blee bah.

Doot doot bah!

Blee blee, doot doot.

Blee! Doot! Wah!

Rat-a-tat, rat-a-tat.

Blam! Bop! Blam!

Boom chicka, boom chicka.

Wham!
Ker-slam!

The music will mix with the trains whirring by.

Sweet sound will abound from the ground to the sky.

A concert like this would be some sight to see—
a movin', groovin', razzin', jazzin'
American jazz symphony!

Chug-a chug-a chug-a chug-a Choo! Choo!
Chug-a chug-a chug-a chug-a Choo! Choo!